Simon's Journey from Unnoticed Genius to True Friendship

Reuel Josh V. Anda

Ukiyoto Publishing

All global publishing rights are held by

Ukiyoto Publishing

Published in 2023

Content Copyright © Reuel Josh V. Anda

ISBN 9789359209746

All rights reserved.

No part of this publication may be reproduced, transmitted, or stored in a retrieval system, in any form by any means, electronic, mechanical, photocopying, recording or otherwise, without the prior permission of the publisher.

The moral rights of the author have been asserted.

This is a work of fiction. Names, characters, businesses, places, events, locales, and incidents are either the products of the author's imagination or used in a fictitious manner. Any resemblance to actual persons, living or dead, or actual events is purely coincidental.

This book is sold subject to the condition that it shall not by way of trade or otherwise, be lent, resold, hired out or otherwise circulated, without the publisher's prior consent, in any form of binding or cover other than that in which it is published.

www.ukiyoto.com

To My Beloved Parents,
Josephine Vargas and John Anda,

Your unwavering love, support, and encouragement have been the guiding stars of my life. Through every chapter of my journey, your belief in me has fueled my dreams and ambitions. This book is a tribute to the profound impact you've had on my life, and it's a reflection of the values and lessons you've instilled in me.

To My Relatives,

Family is the tapestry of love, and you have woven the most beautiful threads into my life. Your presence, wisdom, and shared stories have enriched my understanding of the world and provided the foundation upon which this book stands. I dedicate these words to you with heartfelt gratitude.

Acknowledgement

I want to express my deepest gratitude for embarking on this heartfelt journey through the chapters of "The Unveiling of Authenticity: Simon's Transformation." Your dedication to reading every chapter of Simon's story means the world to me, and I hope you found inspiration and enjoyment within its pages.

Simon's journey, from being an unnoticed genius to a popular and kind-hearted young man, was one of self-discovery, authenticity, and the enduring power of inner beauty. It's a tale that reminds us that true worth lies not in popularity or external appearances but in the authenticity of our character and the kindness we extend to others.

As you followed Simon's trials and triumphs, I hope you discovered valuable life lessons about the importance of self-improvement, staying true to your values, and the profound impact of kindness. His journey serves as a testament to the idea that authenticity and compassion can light the path to a fulfilling and meaningful life.

Your commitment to reading this story is a testament to your own love for literature and the power of storytelling to touch hearts and inspire change. I'm deeply grateful for your time and attention, and I hope that Simon's story has left a positive imprint on your heart.

Thank you for being a part of this journey, and I hope you continue to explore the wonderful world of literature and storytelling

.In the quiet corners of our minds, where dreams and imagination intertwine, we find the essence of storytelling. This tale, penned by a young writer named Reuel Josh V. Anda, invites you to embark on a journey of discovery, kindness, and the pursuit of authenticity. As you turn the pages, may you find inspiration in the unfolding narrative and remember that the power of words can illuminate even the deepest recesses of our hearts. Welcome to a world where dreams take flight and authenticity shines brightly—the world of "The Unveiling of Authenticity: Simon's Transformation."

Index

Chapter 1: The Unnoticed Genius
In the quiet town of Willowbrook, Simon's extraordinary talents and kindness go unnoticed.

Chapter 2: The School Days
Simon's school days showcase his talents and passions, but he remains overlooked by his peers.

Chapter 3: The Glow-Up
Simon's transformative summer sets the stage for his physical and emotional growth.

Chapter 4: The Unveiling
Simon's newfound confidence and appearance capture the attention of his classmates.

Chapter 5: The Unexpected Journey
Simon grapples with the challenges of popularity and the fear of being defined by his looks.

Chapter 6: The True Friends
Simon finds solace in the company of true friends who value his authenticity and inner qualities.

Chapter 7: The Journey Continues
Simon uses his popularity to make a positive impact on his school and community while navigating the complexities of his newfound status.

Chapter 8: The Unexpected Love
Simon discovers love in an unexpected place and learns the true value of genuine connection.

Chapter 9: The Lessons Learned
Simon's journey imparts valuable life lessons about self-acceptance, authenticity, and the power of kindness.

Chapter 10: The Legacy
Simon leaves a lasting legacy of kindness, authenticity, and positive change that inspires his peers and the town of Willowbrook.

Contents

The Unnoticed Genius	1
The School Days	5
The Glow-Up	7
The Unveiling	12
The Unexpected Journey	15
The True Friends	19
The Journey Continues	23
The Unexpected Love	26
The Lessons Learned	29
The Legacy	31
About the Author	*34*

The Unnoticed Genius

In the picturesque town of Willowbrook, nestled among rolling hills and surrounded by lush forests, lived a teenager named Simon. At first glance, Simon appeared to be an ordinary high school student, blending in seamlessly with his peers. He had the same worries about homework and exams, the same hopes and dreams, but there was something truly extraordinary about him that set him apart from the rest.

Simon's brilliance was apparent from a young age. While other children were learning to count, he was solving complex mathematical problems effortlessly. His teachers marveled at his innate ability to grasp even the most challenging concepts with ease. Simon was a true prodigy, a shining star in the world of academics, yet his humility and kindness were equally remarkable.

In the classroom, Simon's hand would shoot up enthusiastically whenever a teacher posed a question. He never hesitated to help a struggling classmate, patiently explaining equations and theorems until they too understood. His classmates admired him for his intelligence and respected him for his generosity, but somehow, Simon remained an enigma to them.

Despite his remarkable talents and kind-hearted nature, Simon was, in many ways, a hidden gem. He rarely sought the spotlight, often opting to spend his lunch breaks in the quiet solitude of the school library, surrounded by books that were his constant companions. While other students gossiped, laughed, and formed groups, Simon found solace in the world of words and numbers.

Simon's favorite spot in the library was a cozy corner where he would lose himself in the pages of thick, dusty tomes filled with mathematical theorems and equations that danced like poetry before his eyes. His passion for mathematics was a source of both solace and excitement. It was a language that spoke to his soul, a world where he felt most alive.

2   Simon's Journey from Unnoticed Genius to True Friendship

One crisp autumn afternoon, as the golden leaves fell from the trees and the soft sunlight filtered through the library windows, Simon delved deep into a book about number theory. Lost in the intricacies of prime numbers and divisors, he was unaware of the world around him. It was at that moment that Emily, a fellow student, approached his table.

Emily was an amiable girl with a warm smile and a penchant for getting to know everyone. She had seen Simon in the library countless times but had never spoken to him before. Curiosity piqued, she pulled out the chair opposite him and said, "Hey, Simon, I've seen you here so often. What are you reading?"

Startled, Simon looked up, his deep brown eyes meeting Emily's friendly gaze. He hesitated for a moment, not used to such direct attention. "Oh, just a book on number theory," he replied modestly, a faint blush coloring his cheeks.

Emily's eyes lit up with interest. "Number theory? That sounds fascinating! Can you tell me more about it?"

And so, an unexpected conversation began, one that would change Simon's life in ways he couldn't have imagined. Emily's genuine curiosity and eagerness to learn drew Simon out of his shell. He found himself explaining the intricate world of numbers, primes, and divisors with enthusiasm, watching as Emily's fascination grew.

As the days turned into weeks, Simon and Emily's friendship blossomed. They spent countless hours in the library, exploring the vast realms of literature, mathematics, and philosophy. Simon's once-hidden genius was no longer confined to the shadows; it had found a voice through Emily, who encouraged him to share his knowledge with others.

One day, Emily approached Simon with an idea. "You know, Simon," she began, "your passion for learning and your kindness are truly exceptional. I think it's time for more people to see the amazing person you are."

Simon was hesitant at first, unsure of what Emily was suggesting. "What do you mean?" he asked.

"I mean," Emily replied with a grin, "it's time for you to shine. To let others see the incredible talent and kindness that you possess. Together, we can make a difference, not just for you but for our entire school."

Simon pondered Emily's words. It was a proposition that both excited and terrified him. The thought of stepping into the spotlight, of sharing his gifts with the world, was a daunting prospect. But he trusted Emily and her unwavering belief in him.

And so, their journey began. Emily and Simon embarked on a mission to showcase Simon's talents and kindness to the entire school. They started by organizing math workshops, where Simon would teach his peers the beauty of mathematics, making it accessible and engaging. The workshops became a hit, and soon, students from all grades were attending.

Word spread like wildfire, and Simon found himself surrounded by eager learners who marveled at his ability to simplify complex concepts. He became a mentor and a friend to many, helping them not only with their studies but also with the challenges of teenage life.

But Simon's impact extended beyond the classroom. He and Emily organized charity events, using their newfound popularity to raise funds for local causes. Simon's kindness was no longer hidden; it shone brightly for all to see. His peers had discovered not only a brilliant mind but also a compassionate heart.

As Simon's presence in the school grew, so did his circle of friends. The same classmates who had once overlooked him now saw him for who he truly was—an extraordinary young man with a gift for knowledge and a heart full of kindness.

The transformation was not just in Simon; it was in the entire school. The atmosphere had shifted, becoming more inclusive and supportive. Emily and Simon had sparked a change that rippled through the student body, creating a community that valued not only academic excellence but also empathy and compassion.

As the school year drew to a close, Simon reflected on his incredible journey from being the unnoticed genius to becoming a beloved figure in his school. He realized that it was his friendship with Emily, her unwavering belief in him, and their shared mission to make a difference that had brought about this transformation.

Simon had learned that true greatness lay not in seeking attention for oneself but in using one's talents and kindness to uplift others. He had discovered that his brilliance and humility were not mutually exclusive but could coexist harmoniously, creating a powerful force for positive change.

In the quiet town of Willowbrook, the story of Simon, the unnoticed genius turned inspirational leader, became a legend. It was a tale of friendship, empowerment, and the extraordinary potential that exists within each of us, waiting to be discovered and shared with the world.

"In the quietest of hearts, the most extraordinary talents often reside, awaiting their moment to shine."

The School Days

Simon's school days were a testament to his remarkable talents and his insatiable appetite for knowledge. Each morning, as the sun's first rays peeked over the horizon, Simon was already up, eagerly preparing for the academic challenges that lay ahead. He had an unwavering dedication to learning, and it was evident in every subject he pursued.

In the realm of mathematics, Simon was nothing short of a prodigy. He could unravel the most complex equations with the ease of a seasoned mathematician. His teachers marveled at his ability to grasp abstract concepts that left others scratching their heads. Simon's notebooks were filled with pages of equations, solutions, and elegant mathematical proofs that hinted at the brilliance within him.

But Simon's talents extended far beyond the realm of numbers. He was a voracious reader, devouring books on a wide range of subjects. Whether it was classic literature, scientific discoveries, or philosophical treatises, Simon absorbed knowledge like a sponge. His thirst for understanding the world around him was unquenchable.

As if being a mathematical whiz and a bookworm weren't enough, Simon had a creative side that was equally impressive. He had a knack for playing musical instruments, with the violin being his instrument of choice. When he drew the bow across the strings, the melancholic strains of his music would fill the air, creating an ethereal atmosphere that seemed to transport listeners to another world. His musical talents were a well-kept secret, known only to a few lucky souls who had the privilege of hearing him play.

Simon's artistic abilities weren't limited to music; he was also a gifted poet. His verses were filled with profound insights, raw emotions, and a wisdom that belied his age. Yet, his poems remained hidden within the pages of his notebooks, a treasure trove of beauty that awaited discovery.

Despite his academic achievements, musical prowess, and poetic talents, Simon's school life was marked by a curious irony. While he excelled in every endeavor he pursued, he often found himself on the sidelines of his peers' social circles. It was as if he existed in a parallel world, where his brilliance and humility were a paradox that left others perplexed.

The girls, in particular, seemed oblivious to Simon's many virtues. Their attention was often drawn to the more charismatic and conventionally attractive boys who effortlessly commanded the spotlight. Simon's modesty and introverted nature made it easy for him to be overlooked, his brilliance hidden beneath a veneer of quiet humility.

But Simon harbored no resentment or bitterness. He was content with his pursuit of knowledge, his love for music, and the solace he found in the world of words. He didn't seek validation from his peers; his validation came from within, from the joy of learning and the satisfaction of mastering new skills.

As he moved through his school days with a quiet determination, Simon remained patient, knowing that someday the world might recognize the extraordinary talents and the kind heart that lay hidden beneath his unassuming exterior. Little did he know that a summer of transformation would soon bring about a change that would alter the course of his life in unexpected ways.

"Education is the canvas upon which we paint the masterpiece of our minds."

The Glow-Up

The long days of summer stretched before Simon like an endless canvas, beckoning him to paint a new picture of himself. It wasn't a desire to impress anyone that fueled his determination; rather, it was a yearning to evolve into the best version of himself. Simon had always been content with who he was, but he sensed that a change was necessary—a transformation that would not only reflect his inner growth but also boost his self-confidence.

It all began with a commitment to physical fitness. Simon joined a local gym, determined to sculpt his body into a form that matched the vitality within him. He approached this endeavor with the same discipline and dedication that had defined his academic pursuits. His goal wasn't to conform to societal standards of beauty but to enhance his overall well-being.

Each morning, before the sun kissed the sky, Simon was at the gym, pushing his limits and breaking a sweat. He embraced weightlifting, cardio workouts, and yoga, recognizing that physical strength was a reflection of mental fortitude. As the weeks passed, his once-slender frame began to gain strength and definition. Muscles, once hidden beneath his unassuming exterior, emerged like works of art.

In addition to his physical transformation, Simon embarked on a journey of self-discovery through fashion. He saw clothing as a means of self-expression, a way to convey his evolving sense of self. Gone were the days of blending into the background; Simon now experimented with different styles, embracing a fusion of classic and contemporary that was uniquely his own.

The local thrift shops and boutiques became his playground. Simon relished the process of selecting outfits that resonated with him, each piece a brushstroke on the canvas of his evolving identity. His wardrobe became a reflection of his newfound self-assuredness, an eclectic blend of sophistication and casual elegance that turned heads and elicited compliments.

Yet, his transformation wasn't limited to the physical realm. Simon recognized that true confidence went beyond appearances. He sought to conquer his shyness and boost his self-esteem, and so he made a bold decision—he joined the local drama club.

The world of acting was unfamiliar territory for Simon, a realm where he had rarely ventured. But he saw it as an opportunity to step out of his comfort zone, to challenge himself, and to develop the kind of confidence that could only be gained by confronting one's fears. Under the guidance of the drama club's passionate director, he embarked on a transformative journey of self-discovery.

Rehearsals became his sanctuary, a space where he could shed his inhibitions and embrace the roles he was assigned. Simon honed his public-speaking skills, learned to project his voice with conviction, and developed a stage presence that captivated audiences. He discovered the power of vulnerability, the ability to connect with others through the portrayal of complex emotions.

The first time he stepped onto the stage in front of an audience, it was as if a new Simon had emerged—a Simon who radiated confidence, who could command attention with the power of his presence. His performances were a testament to his growth, each one a testament to his willingness to push boundaries and challenge himself.

As the summer unfolded, Simon's physical and emotional transformation became increasingly evident. His once-ordinary appearance had undergone a profound metamorphosis, and his newfound self-assuredness shone through in every aspect of his life. The cocoon of self-doubt he had inhabited for so long had given way to the vibrant wings of self-confidence.

The first day of school after summer break was a revelation. Simon walked through the school doors with a newfound sense of self-assuredness that radiated from every step. His physical transformation was undeniable, as his well-defined physique and fashionable attire turned heads and sparked conversations.

But it wasn't just his external appearance that had changed; it was his inner radiance that truly captivated those around him. The self-confidence he had cultivated over the summer had a magnetic quality, drawing people toward him like moths to a flame. His once-reserved demeanor had transformed into an aura of charisma that was impossible to ignore.

It didn't take long for his classmates to notice the profound transformation in Simon. The girls who had never paid him any attention suddenly couldn't take their eyes off him. His male peers, too, were struck by the change and admired the newfound self-assuredness that seemed to envelop him.

Emily, the girl who had first struck up a conversation with Simon in the library, couldn't believe her eyes when she saw him on that first day of school. She had been a witness to his journey of self-discovery, and the change in him was nothing short of remarkable. She approached him with a warm smile, struck by the newfound confidence that radiated from him.

"Simon, you look incredible!" Emily exclaimed, genuinely impressed by his transformation.

Simon's response was a modest but genuine thank you. He appreciated the compliments, but he knew that his journey had been about more than just appearances. It had been a journey of self-discovery and self-acceptance, a transformation that had touched every aspect of his life.

As the school year progressed, Simon found himself navigating the complexities of his newfound popularity. It was a world he had never ventured into, and he approached it with a sense of curiosity and caution. The attention he received was both flattering and overwhelming, and he couldn't help but wonder if people were only interested in his looks.

He grappled with the challenges of balancing his newfound popularity with his true self—the talented and kind-hearted person he had always been. There were moments when he felt the pressure to conform to certain expectations, to maintain a facade of confidence even when doubts lingered beneath the surface.

Yet, through it all, Simon remained grounded. He knew that true beauty wasn't just skin deep, and he was determined not to lose sight of the values and principles that had guided him throughout his life. He leaned on the support of his true friends, those who had seen him for who he was before the transformation, and who reminded him of the importance of staying true to himself.

Amidst the chaos of popularity, Simon found solace in the company of his true friends. They were the ones who had stood by him since the beginning, who had witnessed his journey of self-discovery and transformation. They were his pillars of support, his confidants, and his staunchest allies.

In the quiet moments shared with his closest companions, Simon found authenticity and solace. They were the ones who saw beyond the superficial and celebrated his intelligence, kindness, and unwavering principles. They reminded him that popularity could be a fickle thing, but true friends and genuine connections were the most precious treasures in life.

Simon's journey wasn't just about physical transformation or newfound popularity; it was about a deeper understanding of himself and the world around him. He learned that while outer beauty may attract attention, it was the inner qualities that truly mattered. It was the kindness, integrity, and authenticity he brought into the world that left a lasting impact on those he encountered.

As the school year continued, Simon's popularity became a platform for positive change. He used his newfound influence to promote kindness and inclusivity within the school community. Simon organized charity events, rallied his peers to support local initiatives, and spoke at school assemblies, sharing his experiences and emphasizing the importance of inner growth and self-acceptance.

Through his actions and words, he became a role model for many, inspiring others to embrace their own journeys of self-discovery and authenticity. The school began to shift, as the atmosphere became more inclusive and accepting. Simon's influence reached far beyond the confines of the classroom, touching the hearts of those who had the privilege of knowing him.

Yet, amidst the admiration and attention, Simon remained humble. He understood that his transformation was not about seeking external validation but about embracing his true self. He continued to nurture his passions for mathematics, music, and poetry, finding solace and fulfillment in the pursuit of knowledge and creativity.

In the midst of it all, Simon discovered that popularity could be a double-edged sword. While it brought him closer to the social circles he had once admired from afar, it also came with challenges and expectations. He grappled with the notion that his worth might now be tied to his appearance and the attention he received.

But through self-reflection and the unwavering support of his true friends, Simon found equilibrium. He understood that his intelligence and kindness were assets that should never be hidden, and that he could use his newfound popularity to make a positive impact on his school and community.

The journey of self-discovery and transformation was far from over for Simon. It was a lifelong path, a continuous evolution of self that would shape his character and choices for years to come. He had learned invaluable lessons about self-acceptance, the power of authenticity, and the importance of staying true to one's values.

As he looked ahead, Simon knew that his journey was a testament to the potential for growth and change that existed within each of us. His story served as an inspiration to his classmates and the entire town of Willowbrook, a reminder that inner beauty always shone through and that being true to oneself was the greatest source of strength and authenticity.

"Transformation begins when we choose to be the best version of ourselves, not for others, but for our own growth."

The Unveiling

The first day of school after that transformative summer was a revelation, not just for Simon but for everyone who crossed his path. As he walked through the hallowed halls of Willowbrook High School, there was an undeniable aura of confidence that surrounded him. It was a confidence that seemed to emanate from every pore, a testament to the inner growth he had undergone during those summer months.

Simon's physical transformation was undeniable. His once-ordinary appearance had undergone a profound metamorphosis. His slender frame now bore the sculpted definition of someone who had dedicated himself to physical fitness. Each step he took seemed purposeful, as if he had shed the cocoon of self-doubt that had once enveloped him.

Gone were the days of blending into the background. Simon's fashion choices were a reflection of his newfound self-assuredness. His wardrobe had evolved into an eclectic blend of sophistication and casual elegance, a fusion of classic and contemporary that turned heads and sparked conversations. He had learned that clothing could be a form of self-expression, a way to convey his evolving sense of self.

But it wasn't just his external appearance that had changed; it was his inner radiance that truly captivated those around him. The self-confidence he had cultivated over the summer was like a beacon, drawing people toward him like moths to a flame. He no longer walked with his head down, his gaze fixed on the ground; instead, he held his head high, his eyes meeting the world with unwavering assurance.

It didn't take long for his classmates to notice the profound transformation in Simon. The girls, in particular, who had never paid him any attention suddenly couldn't take their eyes off him. They watched him from the corners of their eyes, their glances lingering longer than usual. The once-unnoticed genius had become a magnetic presence, and his newfound charisma was impossible to ignore.

Emily, the girl who had first sparked a conversation with Simon in the library, was among those who were struck by his transformation. She couldn't believe her eyes as she watched him walk down the hallway. She had been a witness to his journey of self-discovery, and the change in him was nothing short of remarkable.

Unable to contain her excitement, Emily approached Simon with a warm smile. "Simon, you look incredible!" she exclaimed, genuinely impressed by his transformation.

Simon's response was a modest but genuine thank you. He appreciated the compliments, but he also knew that his journey had been about more than just appearances. It had been a journey of self-discovery and self-acceptance, a transformation that had touched every aspect of his life.

As the school day unfolded, Simon's presence was like a breath of fresh air. He exuded a sense of self-assuredness that was contagious, inspiring others to walk a little taller and hold their heads a little higher. The change in him was a testament to the power of self-belief and the capacity for growth that existed within each of us.

Yet, amidst the attention and admiration, Simon remained grounded. He understood that his transformation was not about seeking external validation but about embracing his true self. He leaned on the support of his true friends, those who had seen him for who he was before the transformation, and who reminded him of the importance of staying true to himself.

In the days and weeks that followed, Simon continued to navigate the complexities of his newfound popularity. It was a world he had never ventured into, and he approached it with a sense of curiosity and caution. The attention he received was both flattering and overwhelming, and he couldn't help but wonder if people were only interested in his looks.

He grappled with the challenges of balancing his newfound popularity with his true self—the talented and kind-hearted person he had always been. There were moments when he felt the pressure to conform to certain expectations, to maintain a facade of confidence even when doubts lingered beneath the surface.

Yet, through it all, Simon remained true to himself. He knew that true beauty wasn't just skin deep, and he was determined not to lose sight of the values and principles that had guided him throughout his life. He understood that popularity, while alluring, could be a double-edged sword, and he was determined not to compromise his integrity.

Amidst the whirlwind of attention, Simon found solace in the company of his true friends. They were the ones who had stood by him since the beginning, who had witnessed his journey of self-discovery and transformation. They were his pillars of support, his confidants, and his staunchest allies.

In the quiet moments shared with his closest companions, Simon found authenticity and solace. They were the ones who saw beyond the superficial and celebrated his intelligence, kindness, and unwavering principles. They reminded him that popularity could be a fickle thing, but true friends and genuine connections were the most precious treasures in life.

Simon's journey wasn't just about physical transformation or newfound popularity; it was about a deeper understanding of himself and the world around him. He learned that while outer beauty may attract attention, it was the inner qualities that truly mattered. It was the kindness, integrity, and authenticity he brought into the world that left a lasting impact on those he encountered.

As the school year continued, Simon's popularity became a platform for positive change. He used his newfound influence to promote kindness and inclusivity within the school community. Simon organized charity events, rallied his peers to support local initiatives, and spoke at school assemblies, sharing his experiences and emphasizing the importance of inner growth and self-acceptance.

Through his actions and words, he became a role model for many, inspiring others to embrace their own journeys of self-discovery and authenticity. The school began to shift, as the atmosphere became more inclusive and accepting

"Sometimes, our true radiance emerges when we embrace our inner confidence."

The Unexpected Journey

As the days turned into weeks, and the weeks into months, Simon's life had undergone a remarkable transformation. The once-unnoticed genius had become a central figure in the school's social landscape, and his popularity continued to grow. Yet, amidst the whirlwind of attention and admiration, Simon found himself on an unexpected journey of self-discovery, grappling with the complexities of newfound fame and questioning the nature of the connections he was forming.

Simon's rise to popularity had been as swift as it was surprising. His physical transformation had turned heads and captured the imagination of his peers. The girls who had never paid him any attention suddenly couldn't take their eyes off him. His male classmates admired the newfound self-assuredness that seemed to envelop him. It was a transformation that had elevated him from the sidelines to the center stage of school life.

While Simon appreciated the newfound attention, he couldn't shake a lingering doubt that gnawed at the edges of his consciousness. He couldn't help but wonder if people were only interested in his looks, if the charisma that now surrounded him was merely skin deep. It was a question that weighed on his mind and added a layer of complexity to his newfound popularity.

As he navigated the social dynamics of his school, Simon grappled with the challenges of balancing his external image with the core of his true self. He was, at heart, the same talented and kind-hearted person he had always been. His intelligence and creativity remained his defining qualities, and he had no intention of letting them be overshadowed by his physical transformation.

There were moments when Simon felt a subtle pressure to conform to certain expectations, to maintain the facade of confidence even when doubts lingered beneath the surface. The popularity he had gained came with a set of unwritten rules and assumptions, and he sometimes felt the weight of those expectations bearing down on him.

But through it all, Simon remained committed to his values and principles. He understood that true beauty wasn't just skin deep, and he was determined not to lose sight of the qualities that had defined him from the beginning. He knew that popularity, while alluring, could be a double-edged sword, and he was resolute in his decision not to compromise his integrity.

Amidst the whirlwind of attention, Simon found solace in the company of his true friends. They were the ones who had stood by him since the beginning, who had witnessed his journey of self-discovery and transformation. They were his confidants, his allies, and the keepers of his authenticity.

In the quiet moments shared with his closest companions, Simon found authenticity and solace. They were the ones who saw beyond the superficial and celebrated his intelligence, kindness, and unwavering principles. They reminded him that popularity could be a fickle thing, but true friends and genuine connections were the most precious treasures in life.

One of those true friends was Emily, the girl who had first sparked a conversation with Simon in the library. Their connection had deepened over the months, transcending the superficiality of appearances. Emily saw the real Simon—the kind, intelligent, and passionate young man he had always been.

Their friendship had blossomed into something more, an unexpected journey of emotional connection and mutual understanding. They spent hours together, sharing dreams, aspirations, and the vulnerabilities that lay hidden beneath the surface. Simon had learned that love was not about appearances but about connecting with someone on a deeper level, about sharing a genuine connection that transcended the superficial.

Their bond became a source of strength for Simon, a reminder that there were those who saw him for who he truly was. Emily's unwavering support and belief in him bolstered his confidence, allowing him to navigate the complexities of his newfound popularity with grace and authenticity.

As the school year progressed, Simon continued to use his popularity as a platform for positive change. He organized charity events, rallied his peers to support local initiatives, and spoke at school assemblies, sharing his experiences and emphasizing the importance of inner growth and self-acceptance. His words resonated deeply with his fellow students, and he became a role model for many.

Simon had come to understand that popularity could be a powerful tool for influence and change. He saw it as an opportunity to champion causes he believed in, to promote kindness and inclusivity within the school community, and to inspire others to embrace their own journeys of self-discovery and authenticity.

But even as Simon made a positive impact on those around him, he couldn't escape the complexities of his own emotions. There were moments of self-doubt when he questioned whether his newfound popularity was a true reflection of his worth or merely a result of his physical transformation. He grappled with the fear that he might be defined by his external image rather than the substance of his character.

It was during one such moment of introspection that Emily offered him a perspective that would change his outlook. They sat together by the serene waters of Willowbrook Lake, the sun casting a golden glow on their faces. Emily looked at Simon with unwavering sincerity in her eyes and spoke from the depths of her heart.

"Simon," she began, "I understand that you have these doubts, that you wonder if people are only interested in your looks. But I want you to know something—your appearance might have initially caught people's attention, but it's your character, your kindness, and your authenticity that have truly won them over."

Simon listened intently, absorbing Emily's words. She continued, "You've used your popularity to make a positive impact on this school and community. You've shown that inner beauty always shines through, and that staying true to oneself is the greatest source of strength and authenticity. People see that in you, and it's why they admire and respect you."

Her words resonated deeply with Simon, touching a chord within him. He realized that he had been too focused on the external aspects of his transformation, too preoccupied with the fear of being defined by his looks. Emily's perspective reminded him that his true worth went beyond appearances, that it was the kindness and authenticity he brought into the

"In the dance of popularity, the steps of authenticity are the most graceful."

The True Friends

In the bustling hallways of Willowbrook High School, amidst the flurry of admiration and attention, Simon found solace in the unwavering presence of his true friends. These were the friends who had stood by him since the beginning, who had witnessed every step of his remarkable journey of self-discovery and transformation.

As the whirlwind of popularity swirled around him, it was in their company that Simon felt most at ease. They were the keepers of his authenticity, the guardians of his true self. In their presence, he didn't need to put on a facade or conform to the expectations of his newfound status. He could simply be Simon—the same kind, intelligent, and passionate young man he had always been.

His true friends saw beyond the superficial and celebrated his inner qualities. They understood that while outer beauty may attract attention, it was the inner qualities that truly mattered. It was the kindness, integrity, and authenticity Simon brought into the world that made him remarkable.

One of those true friends was Emily, the girl who had first sparked a conversation with Simon in the library. Their connection had deepened over the months, transcending the superficiality of appearances. Emily had seen the real Simon—the kind, intelligent, and passionate young man he had always been.

Their friendship had blossomed into something more—an unexpected journey of emotional connection and mutual understanding. They spent hours together, sharing dreams, aspirations, and the vulnerabilities that lay hidden beneath the surface. Simon had learned that love was not about appearances but about connecting with someone on a deeper level, about sharing a genuine connection that transcended the superficial.

Emily's unwavering support and belief in Simon bolstered his confidence, allowing him to navigate the complexities of his newfound popularity with grace and authenticity. She reminded him that he was more than just his external image, that his worth went far beyond appearances.

But Emily was not the only true friend in Simon's life. There was Max, his childhood friend, and confidant. Max had been with Simon through thick and thin, and their bond was unbreakable. Max saw Simon for the person he had always been—a brilliant mind with a heart of gold.

It was Max who had encouraged Simon to embrace his talents and share them with the world. He had been there to celebrate Simon's achievements long before the spotlight had turned its gaze in their direction. Max's unwavering support was a constant reminder that their friendship was built on a foundation of authenticity and mutual respect.

Then there was Sarah, a fellow artist who had always admired Simon's talent for poetry. They had spent countless hours discussing the nuances of their craft, sharing their creative journeys, and inspiring each other to push the boundaries of their art. Sarah saw in Simon a kindred spirit, someone who understood the power of self-expression and the beauty of vulnerability.

As Simon's popularity grew, he leaned on the support of his true friends more than ever. They became his refuge in the storm of expectations and scrutiny. In their company, he could shed the weight of his public persona and simply be himself—a young man with a passion for knowledge, a love for music, and a talent for poetry.

It was with his true friends that Simon found moments of genuine laughter and camaraderie. They shared inside jokes, made plans for the future, and reveled in the simplicity of authentic connection. They were his confidants, his allies, and the keepers of his authenticity.

One sunny afternoon, as the school year was in full swing, Simon, Emily, Max, and Sarah decided to take a break from the hustle and bustle of school life. They embarked on a spontaneous adventure to Willowbrook Lake, a serene and picturesque spot on the outskirts of town.

The lake was nestled amidst lush greenery, its waters reflecting the clear blue sky like a mirror. It was a place where time seemed to slow down, where the cares of the world faded into the background. It was the perfect setting for a day of relaxation and reflection.

As they settled by the tranquil waters, the friends shared stories and laughter. Simon felt a deep sense of gratitude for their unwavering support and genuine friendship. They reminded him that no matter how much he had changed on the outside, his true friends valued him for the person he had always been.

Emily, Max, and Sarah expressed their admiration for the positive impact Simon had made on the school and the community. They acknowledged his ability to inspire others to embrace their own journeys of self-discovery and authenticity. But more importantly, they praised him for remaining true to himself despite the challenges of popularity.

"You've shown us that popularity can be a platform for positive change," Emily said, her eyes filled with warmth. "But you've also shown us that staying true to oneself is the most important thing of all."

Max added, "You've always had the brilliance and the kindness within you, Simon. It's wonderful to see others recognizing it too, but remember that we've known it all along."

Sarah nodded in agreement. "Your authenticity is what sets you apart, Simon. Never forget that."

Simon felt a deep sense of gratitude and validation in their words. He realized that his journey of self-discovery had not only transformed him but had also deepened his bonds with his true friends. Their unwavering support and belief in him had been a constant source of strength.

As the sun dipped below the horizon, casting a warm golden glow over the lake, Simon couldn't help but reflect on the unexpected journey he had embarked upon. He had learned that popularity, while alluring, could be a double-edged sword. It could bring admiration and attention, but it could also come with expectations and challenges.

Yet, through it all, Simon had remained true to himself, guided by the values and principles that had defined him from the beginning. He understood that while outer beauty may attract attention, it was the inner qualities that truly mattered. It was the kindness, integrity, and authenticity he brought into the world that left a lasting impact on those he encountered.

As the evening deepened, Simon, Emily, Max, and Sarah watched the stars appear one by one in the night sky. They made a pact to always support each other's journeys of self-discovery, to celebrate each other's authenticity, and to cherish the bonds of true friendship that had carried them through the ups and downs of life.

The unexpected journey of self-discovery had led Simon to a profound realization—that in the company of true friends who valued him for who he was, he had found the greatest treasure of all. It was a lesson that would stay with him throughout his life, a reminder that authenticity and genuine connections were the most precious things in the world.

"True friends are the compass that guides us back to ourselves when we lose our way."

The Journey Continues

As the school year unfolded and the seasons changed, Simon found himself on a path of self-discovery that continued to shape his character and choices. The transformation he had undergone over the summer had been just the beginning, and he was determined to make the most of his newfound popularity while staying true to the values that had always defined him.

Simon had come to realize that his intelligence and kindness were not weaknesses to be concealed but rather assets to be celebrated. They were qualities that set him apart, qualities that made him the person he was. And he understood that it was essential to honor these qualities and use them to create a positive impact on his school and the wider community.

One of Simon's first initiatives was to establish a mentoring program at Willowbrook High School. Recognizing that many students struggled with academics, he saw an opportunity to share his passion for learning and his knack for teaching. Simon recruited a team of like-minded students who were equally committed to making a difference.

Together, they provided academic support and mentorship to their fellow students, helping them overcome challenges in various subjects. Simon's commitment to education and his genuine desire to help others became a source of inspiration for his peers. His once-hidden brilliance now shone brightly as he guided others toward their own academic success.

But Simon's impact extended beyond the classroom. He organized charity drives and community service projects, rallying his peers to give back to the town of Willowbrook. From food drives to volunteering at local shelters, Simon's popularity allowed him to mobilize resources and support for those in need.

In the process, he discovered the power of unity and kindness. Simon's ability to bring people together, to inspire them to make a difference, was a testament to the profound change that could be brought about by staying true to oneself and using one's popularity for a higher purpose.

Yet, the journey was not without its challenges. Simon faced moments of doubt and self-reflection. He questioned whether his actions were driven by a genuine desire to make a difference or if he was merely seeking validation through his good deeds.

In one particularly introspective moment, he confided in Emily, who had become not only his girlfriend but also his most trusted confidant. They sat beneath the shade of a grand oak tree in Willowbrook Park, its branches rustling in the gentle breeze.

"Emily," Simon began, "sometimes I wonder if I'm doing all of this for the right reasons. Am I using my popularity to make a positive impact, or am I trying to prove something to myself or others?"

Emily listened attentively, her eyes reflecting the sincerity of her feelings for Simon. "Simon, I believe that your intentions are genuine. I've seen your kindness and your desire to help others. You're using your popularity as a platform for good, and that's a wonderful thing. But it's also important to remember that self-reflection is a sign of your authenticity. It's okay to question your motives and ensure that you're staying true to yourself."

Simon nodded, finding comfort in Emily's wisdom. He understood that the journey of self-discovery and authenticity was ongoing, and that moments of introspection were a natural part of it. What mattered was his commitment to making a positive impact and his willingness to continually align his actions with his core values.

As the school year continued, Simon's influence reached far beyond the confines of the classroom. His dedication to education and community service had inspired not only his classmates but also the teachers and staff at Willowbrook High School. They saw in him a model student, someone who embodied the ideals of kindness, leadership, and academic excellence.

Simon's authenticity and commitment to his values had created a ripple effect, transforming the school's atmosphere. The once-competitive environment began to shift, as the emphasis on kindness and inclusivity became more prominent. Simon had set a new standard for what it meant to be popular—a standard that placed character and compassion at the forefront.

Through it all, he continued to nurture his passions for mathematics, music, and poetry. He understood that these creative outlets were not only a source of personal fulfillment but also a means of connecting with others on a deeper level. Simon's talents became a bridge, allowing him to forge genuine connections with students who shared his interests.

The journey of self-discovery was far from over for Simon. It was a lifelong path, a continuous evolution of self that would shape his character and choices for years to come. He had learned invaluable lessons about self-acceptance, the power of authenticity, and the importance of staying true to one's values.

As he looked ahead, Simon knew that his journey was a testament to the potential for growth and change that existed within each of us. His story served as an inspiration to his classmates and the entire town of Willowbrook, a reminder that inner beauty always shone through and that being true to oneself was the greatest source of strength and authenticity.

In the chapters yet to be written, Simon was determined to continue his journey of self-discovery and make an even greater impact on his school and community. He understood that popularity was not a measure of his worth, but rather a platform to uplift others and create positive change. With the support of his true friends and the unwavering love of Emily, he was ready to embrace the future with authenticity and purpose.

"Popularity is a stage, but authenticity is the spotlight that never dims."

The Unexpected Love

Just when Simon thought he had unraveled the mysteries of his own transformation and the intricacies of popularity, life had one more surprise in store for him—a twist of fate that would leave him both astounded and deeply touched.

It all began with a casual encounter in the bustling corridors of Willowbrook High School. As Simon made his way through the throngs of students, he felt a gentle tap on his shoulder. Turning around, he was met with a pair of sparkling hazel eyes and a warm, genuine smile.

The girl who stood before him was Grace, a fellow student whom Simon had known but never really interacted with. She had always been on the periphery of his social circles, a friendly face in the crowd. But something had changed.

"Simon," she said, her voice filled with sincerity, "I've been wanting to talk to you for a while."

Simon, slightly taken aback by the unexpected attention, offered a friendly smile and replied, "Of course, Grace. What's on your mind?"

As they began to converse, Simon quickly realized that Grace saw something in him that transcended the external changes he had undergone. She had looked beyond his newfound popularity and glimpsed the genuine person he had always been—the intelligent, kind-hearted, and authentic young man.

Their conversations deepened, and they found themselves spending more time together, sharing their thoughts, dreams, and aspirations. Grace admired Simon's dedication to making a positive impact on the school and the community, and Simon was drawn to her warmth, intelligence, and the depth of her character.

Their connection grew stronger with each passing day, and it didn't take long for them to realize that they had discovered something beautiful—the profound bond of unexpected love. Theirs was a love story that defied stereotypes and clichés, one that captured the hearts and imaginations of their peers.

Simon and Grace's love story became the talk of the school, a narrative that transcended the superficiality of appearances and celebrated the power of genuine connection. Their classmates marveled at how love had blossomed between two individuals who had once moved in different orbits, now brought together by a shared understanding and authenticity.

As Simon reflected on this unexpected turn of events, he came to a profound realization. Love, he understood, was not about appearances or popularity; it was about connecting with someone on a deeper level. It was about finding a soul whose essence resonated with your own, a heart that beat in harmony with yours.

In Grace, Simon had found not only a girlfriend but also a kindred spirit and a confidant. Their love was a reminder that authenticity and sincerity were the cornerstones of meaningful connections. It was a testament to the idea that when two people saw each other for who they truly were, beyond the external trappings, a love story of remarkable depth and beauty could unfold.

Their love also brought a new dimension to Simon's journey. It was a source of inspiration and strength, a reminder that no matter how much he changed on the outside or how popular he became, staying true to oneself and connecting on a genuine level with others were the most valuable qualities one could possess.

Simon and Grace's love story became a symbol of hope and authenticity, inspiring their peers to seek connections that transcended appearances and to embrace the true essence of those around them. It was a love story that defied expectations, reminding everyone that love had the power to illuminate the darkest corners of the heart and reveal the beauty within.

In the chapters that followed, Simon and Grace's love story continued to flourish, deepening their connection and strengthening their resolve to live authentically and with kindness. Their journey together was a testament to the enduring power of unexpected love, a love that had found its way into their lives when they least expected it, illuminating their path with warmth and sincerity.

"Love is not found in appearances but in the depths of connection between two hearts."

The Lessons Learned

As Simon's remarkable journey continued to unfold, it became a wellspring of invaluable life lessons that not only shaped his character but also inspired those around him. The experiences and insights gained along the way served as guiding stars, illuminating the path to a more meaningful and authentic existence.

One of the most profound lessons Simon gleaned from his journey was the importance of self-improvement. He had discovered that personal growth was not solely about external transformations but also about nurturing one's inner self. Simon's commitment to becoming the best version of himself had become a driving force, a reminder that the journey of self-discovery was an ongoing process.

His physical transformation, motivated by a desire to be the best he could be, had been the catalyst for his personal development. Simon had come to understand that investing in one's well-being, both mentally and physically, was an act of self-love. It was a testament to the belief that each individual possessed the power to shape their destiny and become the person they aspired to be.

Staying true to one's values had emerged as another critical lesson. Simon's authenticity had been his guiding light throughout his journey. He realized that authenticity was not synonymous with rigidity; it was a dynamic force that allowed him to adapt to change while remaining anchored in his core beliefs.

Even in the midst of newfound popularity, Simon never wavered from the principles that had always defined him—kindness, humility, and a commitment to making a positive impact. He understood that authenticity was the key to maintaining a sense of self amidst external pressures and expectations.

Kindness had taken center stage in Simon's journey. He had witnessed the transformative power of genuine acts of kindness, both in his own life and in the lives of those around him. The simplest acts of compassion had the ability to create ripples of positivity that touched hearts and souls.

Simon's dedication to making a positive impact on his school and community had demonstrated that kindness was not a passive virtue but an active force for change. He had used his newfound popularity as a platform to uplift others, to bring people together in the spirit of generosity and empathy.

Yet, as Simon navigated the complexities of his journey, he also recognized the dual nature of popularity. It could be a double-edged sword, capable of both elevating and isolating individuals. Simon had learned that popularity, while alluring, could come with expectations and challenges that required a steadfast commitment to one's authenticity.

The allure of popularity had once threatened to overshadow Simon's true self, but he had emerged from that crucible with his integrity intact. He had discovered that the world might admire outer beauty and charm, but it was inner qualities—kindness, intelligence, and authenticity—that left a lasting impact on the lives of others.

The most precious lesson of all was the profound value of true friends and genuine connections. In the chaos of popularity and transformation, Simon had found solace and authenticity in the company of those who knew him for who he truly was. His true friends had been his pillars of support, the ones who had celebrated his journey and shared in his growth.

They had reminded him that no matter how much he changed or how popular he became, the bonds of friendship and the connections formed through authenticity were the most treasured aspects of life. Simon's journey had reinforced the idea that true friends were the ones who saw beyond appearances, who celebrated one's essence, and who stood by one's side through all of life's twists and turns.

"Life's classroom teaches us that the greatest lessons are often learned through acts of kindness and staying true to ourselves."

The Legacy

As the final chapter of Simon's remarkable journey unfolded, it was a testament to the enduring power of authenticity, kindness, and the pursuit of one's true self. His story, once hidden in the shadows, had become a radiant beacon of inspiration for his classmates and the entire town of Willowbrook.

In the end, Simon's legacy was not defined by his popularity or external appearances, but by the profound impact he had on the lives of those around him. He had left behind a legacy that would be remembered for generations to come—a legacy built on the pillars of kindness, perseverance, and authenticity.

His classmates saw in Simon a living embodiment of the idea that inner beauty always shines through. His journey from an unnoticed genius to a popular and kind-hearted young man had shown them the transformative power of staying true to oneself.

Simon's commitment to self-improvement had inspired his peers to invest in their own personal growth, to strive for excellence not for the sake of validation but as a means of becoming the best versions of themselves.

His unwavering dedication to kindness had ignited a wave of compassion in the hearts of his classmates. Acts of goodwill and small acts of kindness had become the norm, creating a school environment that nurtured empathy and inclusivity.

And his authentic spirit had set a new standard for what it meant to be popular. It was no longer about conforming to stereotypes or seeking external validation; it was about being genuine, compassionate, and true to one's values.

Simon's impact extended far beyond the confines of Willowbrook High School. The town itself had been touched by his kindness initiatives and community service projects. The people of Willowbrook had witnessed the transformative power of one individual's commitment to making a positive difference.

As the years passed, Simon's legacy continued to inspire. Students who had once been bystanders to his journey found themselves embarking on their own paths of self-discovery and authenticity. They remembered Simon's story as a reminder that they, too, could overcome obstacles and embrace their true selves.

The town of Willowbrook became a place known not only for its natural beauty but also for its spirit of kindness and inclusivity, a legacy that had been ignited by Simon's journey.

In the heart of Willowbrook Park, beneath the same grand oak tree where Simon had shared moments of introspection with Emily, a commemorative plaque was placed. It bore a simple yet profound inscription:

"In memory of Simon—a shining example of kindness, authenticity, and the enduring power of inner beauty."

As the sun dipped below the horizon on a warm summer evening, casting a golden glow over the tranquil lake, the people of Willowbrook gathered to pay their respects. They celebrated Simon's legacy with smiles and tears, sharing stories of how his journey had touched their lives.

Emily, Max, and Sarah, Simon's true friends, stood together beneath the grand oak tree. They knew that Simon's legacy was not just a memory but a living testament to the enduring impact of authenticity and kindness.

And as the evening deepened, the stars appeared one by one in the night sky, their brilliance a reminder that even in the darkest of times, the light of inner beauty always shone through. Simon's legacy would continue to inspire, a reminder to all that the journey of self-discovery and authenticity was a path worth pursuing—a path that could change not only one's life but also the world.

"Our legacy is not measured by the echoes of our popularity but by the footprints of our kindness and authenticity."

Moral of the Story:

"Our worth is not defined by popularity or external appearances. The true measure of a person lies in their authenticity, kindness, and the connections they forge with others. The journey to self-discovery and staying true to one's values can inspire positive change and leave a legacy that shines brightly, even in the face of adversity."

The story emphasizes that genuine character, staying true to oneself, and cultivating kindness have a lasting impact and create a legacy that truly matters in life.

About the Author

Reuel Josh V. Anda

Reuel Josh V. Anda is a talented teenager with a passion for writing and a dream of becoming an engineer. Born with a vivid imagination and an innate love for storytelling, Reuel discovered the power of words at an early age. Writing became not just a hobby but a way to express ideas, emotions, and dreams.

Inspired by the world of literature and driven by a desire to explore the endless possibilities of storytelling, Reuel embarked on a creative journey that would shape his future. As a young writer, he began crafting stories that resonated with readers, captivating their hearts and minds.

While nurturing his talent for writing, Reuel also harbors a dream of becoming an engineer. His fascination with the world of science and technology has led him to envision a future where he can blend the realms of creativity and innovation, forging a path toward a career that combines his love for storytelling with his passion for engineering. As Reuel navigates the challenges and joys of adolescence, he remains steadfast in his pursuit of both literary excellence and academic achievement. His dedication to his craft and his dream of engineering inspire not only his own journey but also those who have the privilege of reading his words.

In the years to come, Reuel Josh V. Anda hopes to continue honing his skills as a writer, sharing his unique perspective with the world, and ultimately, making his mark in both the literary and engineering realms. His story is a testament to the boundless potential of young talents who dare to dream and work tirelessly to transform those dreams into reality.

www.ingramcontent.com/pod-product-compliance
Lightning Source LLC
LaVergne TN
LVHW041641070526
838199LV00052B/3488